THE
MaSKeR

To my former self at her most afraid

THE
MASKER

Muffled beats in the hallway announce that I've found the party. The Riviera is the only Casino on the strip willing to host a week-long party for crossdressers and trans women. For tonight's event, the organizers have rented the penthouse suite on the top floor of the South tower. A little vestibule separates the hallway from the penthouse, so it's not until I part the beaded curtains at the entranceway that I take in both the scene of the party and the accompanying rush of disappointment.

I will not be finding friends here, and I am dumb for thinking I ever would. I am an eighth-grade girl who has thought she'd find the clique of popular girls at a Tuesday night senior citizen bowling league. I see none of the girls from Facebook, none of the girls who wrote to say that they wanted to go. In fact, I see no one below the age of 40. Everyone already knows each other and looks two to five decades older than I am. Mostly crossdressers, with a smattering of older trans woman, discernable by button noses and buoyant boobs.

The theme of the party is "Lingerie Love;" named after a longtime attendee to the party, Virginia Love, who, unsurprisingly, loved lingerie and passed of a heart attack earlier in the year. On the piano in center of the suite stands a 18" x 24" soft-focus memorial boudoir portrait of Virgina lounging in a red teddy. 1950s rock, the kind that kids dance to at Bar Mitzvah parties, plays from an unmanned DJ booth.

To my embarrassment, quite a few of the cross-dressers recognize me as "that online sissy," even though I'm wearing one of the most demure dresses there—a knee-length black cocktail dress. "Why didn't you wear one of your fabulous sissy outfits?" asks a middle aged woman, wearing a short prom dress, who has decided to be encouraging of what she takes to be a shy girl who needs a little prodding to bloom. "This is exactly the place where you could have worn those ruffles!"

"This is a Diane Von Furstenberg dress," I say, "I wanted to look classy."

A tall trans woman overhears, and laughs, a sort of tut-tut sound. Ms. Prom Queen announces her drink needs refreshing and the tall woman spins on a pair of wedge heels to appraise me. "You can't expect a crossdresser to care about brands," she says, "They dress with their cocks, the shorter the skirt the better. Women dress for each other, which is why I can tell you: that's a nice dress."

"Yours too," I say, although I don't actually like it. A white and black polka dot dress in a funny shape, short enough that you can see the tattoo of a teddy bear on one thigh.

"Thank you, honey. I'm Sally," she says, leaning forward for an introductory cheek-kiss. "Sally Sanslaw."

Her face is ageless, in the way that certain plastic surgeries erase years but don't quite restore youth. The face is familiar to me—I know it—not because I recognize Sally, but because I recognize faces like it, from years of perusing photos of trans women online. It's a Zuckowski face, the work of the plastic surgeon in Chicago who gives all of the trans women who come to him the same pert, one-size-fits-all doll's face, so that his patients resemble fembot sisters of varying heights and colors.

"I'm Krys," I say.

"Good," Sally says, "Now, Krys, tell me something important. Do I have lipstick on my teeth?"

Sally wants to introduce me to another trans woman, Olivia, who founded the party. But as we're threading our way through the crowd, Sally shoots out a big be-ringed hand and grabs my wrist, like I'm about to step out into traffic. "Look at that," she says, "that's some Silence Of The Lambs shit."

She's looking at a very tall, older trans woman dressed like a dominatrix on the other side of the room.

"The outfit?" I'm a little shocked at her reference. The Buffalo Bill character is a real sore spot for trans women. They won't shut up about it online.

"No," Sally corrects me, and pulls me a foot to the left, "Behind her!"

Crossdressers in all sorts of fetish attire fill the room. To me it either all looks like spectacle, or none of it looks like spectacle, so I can't figure out what the

Silence of the Lambs shit might be.

Then I see the masker.

"Oh, shit!" the words come out involuntarily.

"Yeah," says Sally. "Told you."

Eyes holes in a garish motionless face, the barest bump of a ski-jump nose and fat red lips perpetually parted on the cusp of a moan. A bad blonde wig. It takes me a moment to process the costume that hangs from the curves of the silicone suit. It's an abused cheerleader get-up: flared skirt, white top embroidered with the letter C in a collegiate font, but the arm hangs in a sling and a purple circle of makeup smeared on the silicone face approximates a black eye. The masker is alone, at the edge of the dance floor, vamping like a starlet at his reflection in the plate-glass windows, the poreless silicone skin wrinkling and folding at the joints.

"Olivia said he was coming." Sally fumes. "He was on an episode of TLC's *My Strange Addiction*. There were a bunch of female maskers, but the episode focused on him, even though he never took of his mask. I told Olivia to refund his money, but she has no standards. She thinks anyone who registers can come. I didn't go through everything"— Sally waves up and down her body—"to be in the same club with that kind of pervert. But Olivia wouldn't listen."

I'm openly staring. When he turns, two eyes glittering in the mask catch mine. I expect him to stop moving, but he doesn't; he gyrates more, putting on a show for Sally and me, his movements heavy with sexual gratification. I can see nothing beneath the skirt and silicone skin, but from the disturbing knowledge that comes from distinguishing in others the parts of yourself that you most hate, I just know that beneath that silicone suit, his cock is hard.

"If he doesn't stop looking at me, I'm swear I'm gonna punch him," says Sally. For a moment, I tell myself that she's wrong, you can't judge someone, much less punch someone, for enjoying their fetish— but no: this is icky. He is icky. Icky in a way that disturbs me, icky in the ways I suspect the ugliest parts of myself to be. He reminds me of pictures I've taken of myself alone, in outfits that speak to some deep archetypal part of me—my body hidden in ruffles, my hard cock peeping out, my eyes dilated from the pleasure of it. Pink fog, crossdressers call it—the distorting euphoria of dressing, of finally giving in.

Other people are staring at him now too. Some smirking, some disgusted. He turns back to his reflection in the window, running his hands up and down his silicone skin, stripper style, pink fog degassing through the seams of the suit.

This is my first-ever trip to Vegas. I'd never seen the allure until recently, now that I live in the drabbest part of rural Iowa. These days, I'm like a bird for anything shiny and glitzy.

I graduated from college with a bachelor's in American Studies, which everyone had warned me would be useless, and which everyone was right about. I received exactly one job offer: as an archivist at the largest collection of railroad memorabilia in the country, housed at Grinnell College, in Grinnell, Iowa, a small liberal arts school sandwiched into the thin plane between dead-blonde corn and anvil sky.

My last year of college, I barely went out. On Friday nights, while my friends pre-gamed and played beer pong, I camped out in my dorm room with the door locked, jerking off to forced feminization erotica, or browsing fetish clothes on ebay. The prospect of Iowa and the train museum appeared more and more enticing as a retreat, a place to resolve my weird gender shit, to dress up alone and read those forced femme stories, or, better yet, to figure out how to never dress up again, then arrive to some glimmering coastal metropolis triumphant and cured.

But nothing has really changed, except that I'm lonely, and that now, I know so fucking much about trains. Want to know what distinguishes the standard wheel layout on a 1912 ALCO steam locomotive from the company's distinctive "mountain" edition locomotive of the same year? Neither do I. But the difference between the two, I can tell you, is that the 4-8-2 wheel arrangement on the "Mountain" edition was better for pulling heavy loads up steep slopes than the more efficient and standard 2-8-4.

Usually, the most exciting moment of my day comes when I check the messages on the Facebook profile for my girl self. I post a lot of selfies in different outfits on there, and some porny shots too. My inbox is all flattering, pushy letters from men in faraway cities and countries *("hi! i love u shemale lady! walk on me! u do like step on me all over?")*. Last fall, I had around 2,000 followers. But after I got a sissy dress, my follower count exploded.

A Republican fundraiser in Florida sent me the dress. I figured out who he was when a pair of panties he sent me came with a receipt charged to a credit card in his real name. The dress is classic sissy fetish—super-pretty boys dressed in ridiculously feminine satin outfits—frills and bows dripping in a profusion not seen on a cis woman since the fall of the Austro-Hungarian empire. When I opened the box, the ruffles of the petticoat spilled from their confines like over-carbonated soda. Of all the crossdresser fetishes you can have, the sissy fetish is probably the most embarrassing. At least women wear latex and leather, but only sissies wear sissy dresses. Still, the first time I saw myself in it, saw the silhouette I cut in the full short skirt and puffy sleeves, I never wanted to take it off. The dress overwhelms my body. My shoulders, my biceps, my narrow hips? All invisible when I wear a sissy dress. The only thing you see is the most old-fashionedly girly of shapes. There's a kind of safety in it too. You can't even shame me for not looking like a woman, because it's a sissy dress— calling me a faggot or a perv when I wear it is just redundant.

At first, I just wore the dress to read my favorite type of stories: forced feminization erotica on sites like fictionmania.com or nifty.org. All the stories followed the same basic narrative—a powerful person feminizes an ostensibly unwilling male who comes to accept his/her feminization. The stories just swap in an author's preferred fetishes, details, and acceptable degree of coercion. I liked the ones with the handsome men making a boy into a sissy girl. I discovered forced femme stories when I was 13, and have been reading them since. There's 20,000 or so stories on just the website Fictionmania, and my sense of aloneness dissipates when I imagine the sheer volume of people not just writing, but reading, shared versions of my sexuality and fantasies. And then, once I had the sissy outfit, I could suddenly dress like the boys in the stories, not just read about them.

I only had to post a few pics of myself sissified and pouting before some sissy blogs and tumblrs discovered them. I hit the 5,000 friend count allowed by Facebook within a month, and I had to make a page for myself as a celebrity. Then these other girls, also part-time crossdressers, but flirting with transition and porn, with follower counts in the tens of thousands, started liking my photos, commenting on my posts, and chatting with me. The other girls go on and off of hormones that they buy online—trying to sand off their masculine edges and lessen secondary sex attributes, without necessarily altering the fundamental structures of their bodies. But I haven't tried hormones. I don't know if I'm a man, but I just don't really believe I'm a woman—I'm obsessive with my fetishes, about certain clothes, in ways I've never seen in women. I've never heard a girl talk about getting wet putting on a new dress.

In the same way that one might offer to lend a DVD or book, the other girls and I pass each other our gift-buying fans, mostly married men or crossdressers who can't pass and live vicariously through us. I get the sissies and sissy-lovers. After a month or two, I started having phone sex with some of them, which resulted in a closet foaming with ruffles. Finally, I started asking for gift cards to Sephora instead, which I sometime get, but more grudgingly.

I don't really need the clothes—I only ever wear them in my apartment anyway. I just like getting gifts, because something about getting gifts lets me feel my femininity and value in ways I can't access by myself. I get to see myself through the eyes of men and collect material proof that I'm pretty. Like: how pretty did they think I was last week? Six satin panties, a $20 Sephora gift card, and a modcloth.com retro-style dress worth of pretty.

Last Saint Patrick's day, in a Jimmy Johns, a couple of college girls with shamrocks painted on their faces one table over triggered a double despair meltdown: I would never be feminine like them. On top of that, I remembered the previous St. Patty's day, when I went drinking with Johnny, in New York City, back when I was handsome with light stubble and a well-cut wool jacket. Then, it didn't make me feel weird to have Johnny's friendly drunken arm over my shoulders in a way that I know it now would; feeling the weight of it, with my face close to his, imagining what he'd think if he ever saw me in my sissy dress. A combination of grief and disgust at myself welled up and fell as tears into the gross avocado paste that Jimmy John's slathers on their sandwiches, while the shamrock girls carefully ignored my muffled boo-hoos.

I collected myself enough to glance at my reflection in the plate glass window and then had a sense that maybe my tear-stained face looked tragic. The vanity of that assessment cut short my pity-party and I resolved to do more than just dress frilly alone-online.

The next week, some of my Facebook girls told me about a week-long gathering for "trans feminine people" in Vegas. One that actually looked fun: all drinking fruity cocktails and dressing up slutty, none of the panels on voice-training, surgery, or activism that made all other trans conferences seem so deadly. I bought plane tickets that night: one hundred and fifty bucks on Hooters Air, Des Moines to Vegas round-trip, chicken wings included.

O ut on the penthouse balcony, Sally smokes and fumes. "That freak makes me so mad. I'm all woman. I changed everything. I went through so much. And he thinks he can put on a mask and be like me? Have other people think I'm like him? No, I'm not standing for that."

Sally is an ex-DEA special agent who became a professional bowler in a woman's league when she transitioned. None of the other party-goers approach us, except to nod. "Everybody knows I'm a cranky bitch," Sally explains. Sally has been named as one of OUT magazine's trans pioneers. I'm a bit gratified that she sees me as a woman that she fights for, rather than a fetishist like the masker, because firstly, her ire is impressive, and secondly, I wouldn't necessarily see myself as such a sure bet for her team, even though

I'm flattered to be picked.

She's currently enmeshed in a protracted lawsuit with the California chapter of the Professional Woman's Bowling League, who tried to ban her from tournaments on the basis of her being a trans woman. She's had over a decade of harassment, starting from the first time CBS sports featured her on a broadcast. After that, people spat on her. Threw cups of beer at her at bowling alleys. "Who cares when old fat men get all worked up at me?" she's saying, "What kind of losers make women's bowling their crusade anyway? But I've had moms get their daughters, these cute little angels, to come up to me like they were going to ask for an autograph, and then the mom says 'Honey, that's the freak who's ruining women's bowling!'" She coughs, "Said that right to my face—like women's bowling is some china plate I took a shit on. Breaks my heart. I worked hard to be good— " she drops one hand to cup a massive boob, the filter of her lit cigarette pressed to her bust "—I had to relearn my whole approach just so I wouldn't smack myself in the tits every frame."

She had perfected her bowling in a league with her DEA buddies. "That was my life," she said. "You make a bust in the day—you get drunk at the lanes at night. We had a agency league. I was a real bastard. Now I hate the agency, cops, all those types, and they hate me back. But, I'll tell you something," She smirked and tapped my hand excitedly, "I still shoot at the range where cops go—blam blam blam—right on target, so they know what's coming to them if they fuck with me."

She's a good story-teller, one anecdote gliding right into the next, her voice—croaky from what I assumed was tobacco, but turns out to be botched voice surgery—rises and falls for emphasis. Already she's onto the story of how she got outed in her branch of the agency. She had tried to just be a crossdresser. In the early 90s, Ebay auctions freed her to buy as much slutty bimbo apparel as she wanted. Blonde wigs, thigh-high boots, bustiers, corsets, fishnets, the works.

Then one day, one of her DEA buddies asked her if she had an Ebay account, and could she bid on a car he's selling to drive up the price? Sure, she said, and did. Back in those days, other people on ebay could look at the buying history of anyone who bids on your item to verify that they're likely to pay. Her friend looked at buying history. "I got a call in the middle of the night," she said, "Got told not to show up at work, that faggot trannies get what's coming. I called in sick for a week. Finally, I called one of my friends, and he called me a faggot too, but his wife talked to me. She told me that word about me was already out."

That next weekend, the Los Angeles division of the DEA held their yearly Christmas party. They had rented a karaoke machine, and each department nominated a couple of guys to develop an act. 300 DEA special agents and their wives sat facing the stage when Sally sauntered in dressed in a sexy Mrs. Claus outfit—the red velvet mini-dress trimmed in faux-white fur and knee-high black leather boots. 600 eyes of the law trained themselves on Sally.

"Isn't someone going to buy a girl a drink?" Sally asked to a silent room. No one said anything, and finally her superior said, "Someone get him a drink." She downed the whiskey handed to her, marched up to the stage, picked up the microphone, and sang a rendition of Nancy Sinatra's *These Boots Are Made For Walking* a capella, because of course no one moved to cue up the song when she asked for it. To hear her tell it, you could've heard a pin drop. Then she announced her resignation from the force and cat-walked out. "My bitch ex-wife got half of everything. I even had to sell the '57 Chevy hot-rod I restored, but I sold it super cheap so she'd get half of almost nothing. And half of it for me was still enough to buy Miss Muffin."

"Miss Muffin?"

"That's what I named my pussy. She's real pretty. I showed her to my cousin, and she said mine looked better than hers."

The badass Christmas party story impressed me—but c'mon, *Miss Muffin?* I must have made a face.

"You'll have one too." She assures me, "I can tell—you in your little DVF dress. You're the type that's gonna want one real bad real soon."

The Miss Muffin thing weirds me out. As does the idea of anyone thinking about my potential vagina. "I don't think so," I said, "I mean, no offense, but I'm not dysphoric about my junk. I think I'm all right just being a crossdresser."

She scoffed. "Look, you want to end up like them in there?" She jerked a thumb at the cross-dressers inside the suite. "I don't think so. I'm a real woman. And I'll bet my left tit that you're gonna want to be one too."

A tall man, with wavy dark hair, glinting stubble, and a well-fitting light grey suit, sits next to me at a blackjack table to which I've escaped the party and Sally's hectoring about my womanhood. The guy looks like Superman, if Clark Kent had gotten into ballet instead of Kryptonic steroid abuse. I've only played blackjack twice before, but I'm up thirty dollars—which, for once this week, makes me feel like a cosmic winner. Then, on the first hand I play next to Superman, I go bust. He tsks at me.

"You should have split your cards," he said.

I don't actually know what it means to split my cards. I glance at the dealer. She holds my look, but her face stays flat and impassive. I want to ask the rules of splitting, but since it's been imprinted on me that everyone in Vegas will shark me, I'm afraid of letting her, the room, the cosmos, know that I don't even know the rules of the game on which I've put money.

"What will you drink?" The skinny superman asks me, and snaps at a passing cocktail waitress, somehow elegantly, in a way that made me think he must be European.

"Nothing, thanks."

"Nothing to drink? Every trans woman that I've ever met has been a dedicated alcoholic. But not you?"

A heat passes through my chest. I know I don't pass to anyone who looks at me longer than a minute or two—but he sees me as a trans woman, rather than just a crossdresser. Maybe I don't pass as a woman, but at least it looks like I eat their hormones. "No, I'm not an alcoholic," I say, grasping for hauteur, "My vices are emotional."

Superman laughs, "Here's a tip: a line like that is a dead-giveaway that you're an innocent. Old cynics know to at least fake naiveté." Some sort of slight accent—a generic European sophistication—gives extra weight to his appraisal. I can't think of a good response. Superman orders a whiskey and then he and the dealer, who paused while he ordered, exchange some rapid Spanish—he's one of those men, apparently, for whom all women's actions politely cease when his attention wanders elsewhere—and only when he focuses back on her, does she resume flicking out a new set of cards. He slides his cards off the table with a hand that looks manicured, the motions so gliding that his limbs appear nearly without joints. Without averting his glance from the cards, that same hand gracefully deducts a short stack of chips from a larger one, and tosses it onto the felt for a bet.

I spin on the stool and look at him openly. He must be in his mid forties—his skin tan and slightly sunburned, like he spent the day at a pool, and there are asterisks of wrinkles at the corner of his eyes, the irises of which look like candy-bar caramel against the sunburn. "Are you negging me?" I ask

"I'm sorry, negging?"

"The pickup artists' trick. Where you subtly insult a girl to make her focus her attention on you, prove you wrong."

When he speaks, his tone has changed, now earnest and almost fatherly. "No, I'm not negging you, I am flirting. I called you young and offered you a drink, because yes, I would like to pick you up."

He picks me up. It's thrilling. He takes me to the Voodoo Lounge on the top floor of the Rio Casino, and we sit on the deck, hundreds of feet up, where I catch a reflection of myself in the dark glass, and can't quite believe how glamorous I look. The desert breeze toys with strands of my wig, presses my skirt to my legs and lets it spinnaker behind my ass, while a slim, besuited Superman gently steers me by the elbow, as he might the tiller of a sailboat in a light wind. Felix is his name, an Argentine doctor, an OB/GYN, now living in Los Angeles. Even the cis women, the tall beauties in bandage dresses, can't seem but to appraise him and pass hopefully close, their unfamiliar envy more soothing to me than even the balmy breeze.

He's honest with me. He's got a wife and daughter back in L.A., but he likes trans women. He comes to Vegas every few months. Sometimes he goes to the Las Vegas Lounge and picks up a girl for the weekend and they pretend they are a couple. "I've been living in this country for twenty years," he said, "but my wife is Argentine too. And she would never understand. Maybe if I had grown up here, I would have married a transsexual. We Argentines get mocked as the last holdout of Freudian psychoanalysis, but actually we're repressed about what we want." I laugh knowingly, even though I've never heard this stereotype, much less made fun of an Argentine for it. Maybe someday I will.

He shows me pictures of his house on his phone. It's taken from a lounge chair in the back yard, like one those shots that girls take of their thighs at the beach, only instead of the tanned hotdog legs and ocean, there's a pair of trousers tipped in oxblood leather brogue shoes, set against a very blue pool in the foreground and a view of the hills outside L.A. backdropping the scene.

He tells me that I'd make a good wife, that I'm funny, that I cast my eyes down shyly when I laugh. The idea of myself as a wife, of belonging to a man like this, makes me feel demure, vulnerable, and turned on. I'm suddenly very aware of my nipples.

"I want to take you shopping tomorrow," he proposes, then holds up a hand, as though I'm about to interrupt, when already I'm nodding enthusiastically. "I know, it's very *Pretty Woman*. But one of the fun things about girls like you is how excited you get over clothes. My wife, she doesn't like to dress up for me like that. I love shopping with the girls I meet here."

I squeeze his hand in a yes. This is why I've spent so many cold Iowa nights under the covers touching myself: my online sissy fantasy Daddy come to life.

He appraises my dress. "If you like designer dresses, we can go to some of the high-end boutiques, but—" he pauses, and beckons me forward with a finger, and when I lean towards him he says softly, "—I want you to wear a pair of sheer panties. I want your cock on display to me through your panties every time you change clothes."

I'm in so much pink fog, it's as if 1850s London were a city in Candyland.

Felix and I get out of the taxi back at the Riviera. Even at 3:30, guests line the taxi queue. Felix is in charge, paying the taxi, tipping the valet. I let myself daydream about the movie *Casino*, where in a voiceover, Robert De Niro muses that the taxi valets are the most connected men in Vegas, the men who knew who arrives with whom, who has drugs, the destinations of the cars into which climb starlets and high-rollers.

"Hey!"

I think about Sharon Stone in that movie, with her short dresses and the long blonde 70s hair bound up in a high-pony. That Vegas hustler girl she played, in love with a skeezy con man, taking the casino Mafioso men for a ride, even as they constantly humiliated her. Ever since Felix told me that he wanted to see me in sheer panties, he's been calling me Princess. The men in the forced femme stories always call their prey Princess. And the sissy-lovers online also call me Princess. But the word is more intense in real life—people overhear, and each time feels like I'm being complimented and put in my place all at once.

"Hey!"

This is a glamorous moment, the first taste of a future me. A handsome man is coming back to my hotel room. Tomorrow, he's going to dress me up, make me his prize. Felix puts his hand on my lower back, one finger tracing the top of my panties through the fabric of my dress. I press into him coyly, Sharon-Stone style.

"Hey! Rubber boy!"

Felix's hand stops its panty-exploration. There's a large woman staring at me, waving her hand to get my attention. Some lizard part of my brain processes that she's trans, even before I recognize her as Sally.

"You going somewhere with him?" she demands. She's angry and intimidating. I suddenly see how she could have been a bastard cop. A big French-tipped hand points at Felix. The partiers in line for a taxi titter and glances bounce from the Sally to me. Any sense of glamour seeps away as anticipation crackles through drunken taxi line: *tranny fight!*

Instead of walking around, Felix reaches to

unclip the velvet rope for the taxi queue, fumbles with the clip, and then annoyed, steps awkwardly over the fuzzy-caterpillar part of the partition. He's talking as disentangles his legs, "What is your problem with me?" It's the first time all night I see him lose his grace.

"My problem is that you're a pervert. My problem is that you don't belong here. You're not part of our sisterhood."

That Felix is not part of any sisterhood seems obvious to me, still standing in the taxi queue with an audience of strangers. Sally points at me again. "My problem is that now I see you snatching off the youngest girl at the party," her volubility falters and she waves her hand, "for whatever *Silence of the Lambs* shit you're into."

There it is again. *Silence of the Lambs.* And then, abruptly, like two film slides superimposed over each other, I see the match. With the source film revealed, Felix is revealed as well. His manicured hands, which I had found sophisticatedly European, now obviously feminine. His slim figure, no longer dashing, but fey and cephlopodan. Those glittering eyes, now cold. The masker.

I'm on the other side of the velvet rope without even knowing how I got there. My dad's eyes pop out unattractively when he's affronted, and although I've never seen myself angry, I've heard mine do too. "Did you follow me to the blackjack table?" The accusations sputter out of me. "You were staring at me at the party! You followed me! You tricked me!"

Sally closes in with me. "What were you planning to do with her? Make yourself a real skin suit?"

A confused laugh barks out from the taxi queue. The masker—"Felix" now seems like a disguise, a costume he put on for me—cocks his head, at me, almost morosely. "How could I trick you? I was only nice to you," he says. "I didn't lie to you; I tried to be what you wanted."

"Leave her alone." Sally says.

And then, the masker's expression sours, and his voice lowers into a snarl, "You leave me alone, you freak. You've hounded me since before I even showed up."

Sally tuts, a dismissal.

The masker points at her face, sneers, and observes, "At least I can take my masks off. You're botched plastic surgery Barbie forever."

Her inhale is audible. With that, he's away, pushing out across the parking lot, while the taxi queue gawks, with mounting disappointment, at the two trannies who neglect to fight each other.

I'm awake, disoriented in an unfamiliar hotel room, the crusts of old makeup stinging my eyes. On the far side of the king bed lies Sally, her long red hair waterfalling over the pillows, beer-bottle-green eyes watching me. She croaks out a good morning and lights a cigarette. Her room is bigger than mine, white sunlight hitting a balcony beyond a gauzy curtain. The night before plays through the cracked lens of my mind's projector, and I say thank you to her, recalling her rescue, and then my attempts to calm her down after she confronted Felix, attempts that ended up with me falling asleep in her room. She seemed so sad, so lonely, and so grateful when I offered to sleep there.

"I got a T-shirt you can wear, and some shorts, if you don't want to do the walk of shame back to your room," she says. She won't let me thank her, cuts me off to insist that sisters look out for each other. She decides that she'll take me around for the day. That she's my big sister has become a fact, without my really acceding to it.

"Everything on the Vegas Strip is overpriced," she says, lighting another cigarette and opening the door to her balcony, "You get washed and changed. I have a car. We can go into the real Vegas. We'll have some wonton soup for lunch and then I'm going to get my hair styled. You come with and we'll see what Lety—that's the girl who does my hair—can do for you. She's in a place far from the strip—it's called Curl Up And Dye, isn't that cute?"

I tell her that I wear wigs, but she shakes her head, like I've said something childish, "There comes a day where you have to give that up. Every girl should wear her own hair—you let Lety work on you today." She regards me. "Even in your boy clothes, she'll know you're a girl."

I've got blonde highlights now, and my hair has a pixie look to it—I keep wanting to examine it in the reflection of my phone. But in the dark of the Tiki Bar, the faux thatch ceiling dimly illuminated only by the light of digital poker machines, I can't make out any detail. I cried when I saw my hair—out of happiness, actually, the whole salon experience, treated like a woman in a room full of women, the way Lety fussed over my hair, and how she took for granted that I'd want the blonde to bring out the flecks of gold in my eyes, that she even noticed those flecks, in the way that I've seen women instinctively notice and appraise each others' attributes—all of it added up to waterworks when she passed me a hand mirror to examine my hair from all sides. Sally started to cry too, and then Lety teared up—then all these salon girls, tattooed Latinas—going "awww."

Now at the Tiki Bar, she's drinking out of a souvenir cup in the shape of a Tiki Head. She collects them, and you can only get them by ordering cocktails at this bar, she insists. A picture on her phone shows an entire shelf of them, in a cramped room decorated in the color scheme of Malibu Barbie's Dream House. The photo hurts my heart. As does almost everything else she says as she gets drunk. She has plans to take me to Victoria's Secret once I start hormones, which she has taken as a given that I have been dying to do, because, she says, every girl dreams about her first trip to VS. I imagine some poor sales girl scoffing to her friends, after fitting me for a bra with giant Sally watching and prattling on about her little sister. The thought of it makes me hate myself, hate how I'm saddled with a stupid fetish or gender or whatever that constantly slowly compels me to rob myself of any dignity. It also makes me sort of hate Sally.

Sally talks the bartender into selling her three souvenir cups without having to buy cocktails. To me, it seems like he agrees in order to not have to talk to her anymore, but when he turns away, she strikes am ultra girly coquettish pose, bent at the wrists with her nails under her chin. "I always get the cute girl discount!"

It's all I can do not to point out that she's in her sixties.

Next, she tells me what kind of dress to wear when I next see my parents. "You have to show them your womanhood," she advises. "They have to see it. Otherwise they'll never accept that it's true." Then she offers to talk to my parents for me. She says she's great with mothers.

I recoil at the idea. I've never seen my mom wear makeup. And although she makes her living as a corporate lawyer whose main function seems to be telling any opposing male counsel to go creatively fuck himself, she has the disdain for femininity of second-wave feminism without the accompanying sense of female solidarity. When I brought home my first girlfriend, who wore for the occasion eyeliner and a shirt that revealed her bra straps, my mom beckoned me into the other room and told me, loudly enough for my girlfriend to overhear, to keep my hussies out of both her house and my little sister's sight. My mom would dismiss Sally as a grotesque of womanhood, a cautionary example of man's own sexist fantasies overtaking him. Were Sally to approach her to suggest that her only son become exactly that sort of grotesque, my mom would open the floodgates holding back the malice and bitterness that she usually only lets trickle into her work and family life.

"I think it's better you stay far away from my mom," I say.

Even in dim light, I can see Sally jerk back, as though I had slapped her. "It's just that my mom is kind of a bitch," I add, to soften my reaction.

"Don't talk about your mother that way," Sally snaps. "You don't know when she'll be all you have."

We don't say much for a few minutes. Rockabilly music plays, and with every sip of my vanilla-flavored drink, I can smell the lingering odor of the products in my hair. Finally, Sally says, "I have a plan for that creepy masker. I know you'll want to help."

She orders one more drink for each of us—

mine is in a teal Tiki mug that will round out this year's collection—and lays out her scheme. Thursday night—two nights away—is the night of the party buses. All the crossdressers and trans women put on outrageous outfits, pile into neon-lit party buses with stripper poles and open bars, and drive around from casino to casino, making grand entrances and flash mobbing the gaming floors with trannies. It's supposed to be the most fun night of the whole week.

To prevent robbery or cheating, it's illegal to wear a mask in any casino in Vegas, says Sally. "It's useful being an ex-cop. I know all the laws here, and I checked up on it." The Riv knows that there are CDs all over, Sally explains, but the other casinos don't. According to Sally, the Cosmopolitan in particular really hates trans girls—they got sued for kicking out trans women who use women's bathrooms. "It's the newest place on the strip, their whole thing is being classy. That's the place that really won't want a masker inside. They already want to harass us, but they don't have the right." She puts her hand lightly on my arm for emphasis. "But they can legally arrest the masker. He'll be charged with a felony."

"That seems kind of harsh." I say.

Her hand on my arm tightens. "Girl, you

don't understand men yet. He probably would have raped you."

The accusation lands like an alien. Vaguely, I understand intellectually that I am rapeable, but the possibility isn't an emotional reality for me. But Sally goes on. "That freak is not a woman. He uses us. He uses our struggle so he can get off on his perversions. You understand? We struggle! People spit on me! They boo me! But I still show up at the lanes, to prove that I deserve my womanhood. That you deserve yours! I don't do it so some freak can put on a mask and rape young girls."

The couple beside us, blond Midwestern types, whip their heads around at her outburst. Sally glares back. For a second I think she's going to insult them.

"So you're going to call in an anonymous tip or something?" I ask, willing her attention back on me. "Have security waiting and on the look-out for a masker?"

"Not quite," says Sally, "Everyone already knows that I hate the masker. I threw a fuss when he signed up for this. I need an alibi. So that's why you have to call in the tip."

It's 8:00 P.M. and an indoor sun appears to be setting over the gently ruined Italianate shops, painted pink clouds floating completely still overhead, and everyone shopping looks gorgeous in the golden light. I know it's an illusion, and I know that I should find the illusion cheap—but the indoor Venetian walkway at The Forum Shops at Caesars's are blowing my mind. I know that everything in Vegas is a replica, but the Forum shops are more like my fantasy of Venice than Venice could ever be: the sunlight always hovering at the golden hour, cars never having been invented, the aging streets gleaming spotlessly, and a man who looked like a fashion magazine's idea of Italian masculine beauty guiding me gracefully along. Felix, holding my hand, really looked amazing.

He'd knocked on my door in the late afternoon. "Hey Princess," he said, when I swung open the door, "Can I come in?" It was like the end of last night hadn't happened. He wanted to take me shopping, just as he had promised. He'd seen a black body-con style dress in one of the windows, and he couldn't wait to see me try it on.

It's the "Princess" that does it. The whole thing perfectly followed the scripts of the forced feminization erotica stories I'd been reading my whole life. I knew my role, and whatever realities actually existed between me and him, whatever plot Sally had for us, whatever thing Felix did with his masks, I wanted to put it all out of my mind. The Odyssey might the foundational text for Western culture, but forced femme erotica is the foundational text for closeted crossdressers, and I'm erotica-literate enough to know that the stories only get hot when authors don't mess up the basic narrative: when a man calls you Princess and wants to dress you up, a sissy will blush and defer to his strength.

Felix sets down on a bench a shopping bag from Marc Jacobs, inside of which lies wrapped a cute dress in a flowered pattern. It's not what I would have chosen for myself, but half the fun was in letting Felix dress me, being a man's dress-up doll, having him tell the clerk at the store, with complete confidence, which dresses he wanted me to try on, and watching how she, in the face of Felix's confidence and AMEX, maintained the conceit that it was perfectly natural for him to have brought in a boy to try on the dresses. I barely had to speak—Felix said he'd only take me to the more expensive stores, where the commissions were high enough no one would care who's buying.

At my hotel room, he had insisted that he hadn't followed me last night, and I believed him. Now, he stops me, and points to Agent Provocateur. Quietly, he says, "I want to buy you those sheer panties, Princess. You'd love that, wouldn't you."

I meet his eyes and nod.

"Then say you're sorry."

I want to pull back slightly, but his grip is tight on my arm. Fear lightly twangs the strings of my nerves. Not fear that he will hit me, but fear that he will somehow humiliate me in this ersatz Venice. "I don't…I don't understand. Sorry for what?"

"For last night. You judged me. You accused me."

"I thought you had followed me. I felt tricked."

"That's not an apology." His eyes narrow and his crow's feet lengthen. I don't know him very well, but the twanging increases.

"I'm sorry. I shouldn't have accused you or judged you."

"That was pretty hypocritical of you, wasn't it? You're a little pervert sissy faggot, aren't you? You think you have the right to judge me?"

The words sting, especially since they come when I'm in the fanciest mall in Vegas, vulnerable and dependent on him. I gather myself, remind myself that no one can talk to me that way, but as I do, he smirks slightly, and suddenly, I realize that he's both deadly serious about the apology, and that this is a sexual game.

"Yes," I pause, but I say what I know he wants, "I'm little pervert."

"And a sissy faggot."

"And a sissy faggot." People are walking right by us. I try to keep my gaze on him, try to not to look to see if they've heard.

"Yes, you are. You don't know anything. That's why you need a man like me to take care of you. Now tell me, Princess, I bet you need a new pair of panties, don't you? I bet yours just got all wet."

He's right. I'm hard. Gaggles of tourists walk by and I'm standing there with my clit, or cock, or whatever, straining against the light fabric of my drawstring pants, as nervous and turned on as I've ever been. I try to arrange my satchel, the purse that could pass for androgynous, to cover my crotch. Felix slides his hand down my arm, and for a second, I both fear and hope that he's going to touch me there. I can't tell if it's me, or if the amazing sunset-emulating lights have changed slightly, but everything—the glitzy store fronts, the plaster ruins, Felix's skin tone, have all gotten richer, more saturated and vivid. My senses are awake like they've never been, like some I'm some kind of tropical prey, holding dead still, but taking in torrents of unprocessed sensory stimuli as a panther pads softly by. Felix doesn't touch me, instead he pulls away my satchel and places it at my side, revealing the hard-on barely hidden in the tent of my pants without ever touching it. Then the sex and menace in his stance recede.

"I know my masking is new to you. But don't you understand that it's because I have fetishes too that I know so well how you need to be treated? You're a lucky girl that you met a masker."

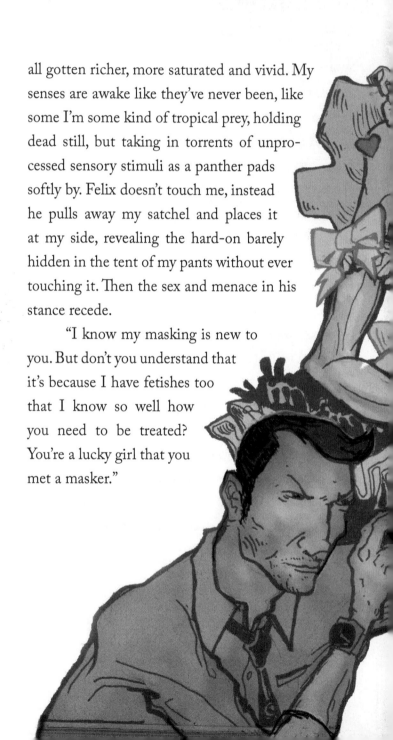

I apologize again, and tell him that I'm sure he's right, that I'm lucky. He reaches down, and lightly, so that almost no one could catch it, pats the tent of my linen pants. "All right, Princess. Now you're in the right condition to try on those panties for me."

F elix has parked his BMW up on a pullout on the highway up to the Red Rock Canyon. Below, darkened patches at the outskirts of the city mar the messy grid of Vegas streetlights, where only a few houses in the failed developments of the housing boom are illuminated. My mouth tastes like semen. Up until 10 minutes ago, I didn't really know what a man's semen tasted like, but now my mouth is thick with the flavor, and I'm still not sure how to describe what it actually tastes like, but it won't go away, no matter how much I swallow. Felix is talking about those abandoned developments, but I'm barely listening. I'm focused on my internal monologue, like I'm split, my one half of consciousness outside myself, talking to the other half, which is inside of me, but quiet, listening and emoting as it's lectured. *Krys, you're a cocksucker now*, is what the part outside of me keeps saying. The part of me inside my body, listening, wants to be ashamed, but is instead helplessly excited at each repetition. *Krys, you blew a man in his car while he spanked your pantied ass. Krys, you are officially a cum-eating whore. Krys, this man bought your slut mouth for the price of a dress.* And then, weirdly, *Krys, now you will never be president of the United States.*

I jump. Felix has pinched my thigh. "Are you listening to me, Princess?"

"Oh, I spaced out—a little dazed."

He leans over and puts one finger under my chin, gently turning my head towards him. "A little ditzy. That's cute. But I was just saying that you're an ungrateful bitch."

"What? Why?"

Did I do it wrong? Was I bad at it?

"Because you're wasting a gift."

I couldn't think of anything he'd given me that I'd wasted. But he went on, "Almost everyone at that party is wasting a gift. The trans women especially." His fingers find mine and intertwine. I'm dismayed how his grip reveals that how much thicker my hands are than his. I have very stout hands, unfortunately. I am a terror to play "Mercy" against.

"Let me tell you something." It's dark enough

in the car that I mostly see his profile in outline. He doesn't wait for my assent. "I'm in private practice now, but about five years ago, I was working in a public hospital in L.A. I saw a lot of horrible things. Always on call, delivering premies for mothers who'd just as soon have let the baby die. There was a lot of burnout among doctors, there's NA and AA meetings just for MDs. But I was always known as very calm, very together, very reliable. I'm that way as a husband too. You know why?"

I understood that I was supposed to answer. "No, why?"

"Because on the bad days, I went home and put on a female mask, and I felt sexy and relaxed and at peace. Do you know what a gift that is? Normal people, they have to drink alcohol, they have to take cocaine, to kick their dogs, and bully their wives, or punch strangers at bars. But you and I have a super-power. You can just go home and put on a sissy dress. But you're not grateful for your gift. You think it means something is wrong with you, that you should be a woman. Actually, you are as you were intended to be. Every transsexual I have met has wasted their gift and picked up so many worse habits to replace it. But our gift can bring us joy."

In the dark, I feel his hand drop mine. Lightly he traces the outline of my clit through the panties he got me with the back of his nails. I haven't come yet, and almost instantly, my body responds. I like what he's saying. I've told myself similar things so many times. Why can't I just let my crossdressing be a fetish? What if I was just unashamed of it, and let it be a small, contained, but important part of my life? What if I just owned it? If I told my friends— hey, this is something I like and do alone—same as anything they're into. Why does my particular fetish have to take such precedence that I change my whole life, my whole body, just to accord with it? Why can't it be a gift just as it is?

"Everything is in balance for me." Felix is still toying with me. "You've seen pictures of my house and pool. I love being a father—I taught my daughter to play soccer, and she's varsity even though she's only a freshman. My parents back in Argentina get to be grandparents. You understand? It's a good life," I'm grinding my pelvis back against his hand and Felix is saying, "I take care of my family, and I have my little escapades. My favorite is when I can share them with someone like you. I want more with you. You're so pretty. Men will want you just as you are. If you embrace yourself, you'll always have people to share yourself with. But you listen to someone like that plastic surgery nightmare you were with the other day, and you'll end up like it."

The "it" startles me out of my lust. A wrong note played against the rhythm of his stroking. I picture Sally. The way she cried for me when I showed off my hair. "She hates you," I say.

"Yes, I know." His hand goes still. "Sally has been threatening me online since I signed up for this week. She appears to be a very lonely and sad person."

"Yes, but don't underestimate her."

"Why would you say that? Why would I need to estimate her at all?"

I want his smooth hand back on me. "Okay," I say, "but don't get mad, she was just talking." And then I tell him about her plan, how she figured out it was illegal to wear masks in the casino, and how she wanted me to call in a tip.

"I wasn't really going to report you," I assure him, although I hadn't really decided until I remembered her plan just now. "I just listened to her vent because I thought you had tricked me. But maybe it's actually good that she still wants me to call it in, because I can say I will, and then she'll miss her chance." I feel pretty satisfied with this explanation. It positions me as his savior.

Abruptly, he flips on the overhead lamp, and the car floods with light, a fishbowl illuminated in the black of the desert foothills. I'm just wearing the panties he bought me, exposed to any driver that happens to pass by. As I reach for my shirt, my arms half caught in the folds of the fabric, Felix's hand flashes out and slaps me. "You stupid faggot," he hisses.

I've never been slapped before. The cracking sound shocks me less than the disbelief that he's touched me.

"You could ruin my life," he says.

I stare at him, cradling the left side of my face in my palm, instinctively, arms still only half in my shirt. He slams a fist on the leather steering wheel and I flinch. "Do you understand what you're playing with?" His voice goes high, "I deliver babies. Do you know what that arrest would do to me? To my family?"

I barely hear him. The sting recedes, replaced by outrage. "I thought you were bragging how you're so calm, so peaceful," My tone is as sarcastic as I can manage. "Maybe you need to put on your mask again."

"Get the fuck out of my car."

I don't have my pants on. We're in the middle of nowhere. I look at him in disbelief.

"Get the fuck out!" The shout is so loud in the quiet. And now I am scared. I see myself alone, with my new highlights and panties, walking in the desert night.

"Wait. No. I'm sorry." I say. "I'm really sorry."

He reaches over, and I raise my hands in defense, but he leans past me, pulls the door handle, and the BMW door releases with a lush luxury sound and swings smoothly ajar. He points.

"Please. I'm really sorry. I didn't want Sally to do it, that's why I told you."

He starts the car. After a moment, he puts the car in reverse. "You did tell me," he says quietly, "And for that, I'll drive you back. Close your door."

Felix slurs the car through dark curves, pulling my stomach with the force. Heat flushes the left side of my face. The moment of the slap loops in my thoughts. He slapped me as I had seen women slapped in movies, by brutes larger than them, without fear or consideration that the woman might retaliate. Assured of her physical helplessness. But I am not that much smaller than Felix. My hands are larger. Yet I took the slap without even thinking of hitting back, had even apologized, meek as an abused woman. Whatever size I might be, whatever shape, Felix saw me as a woman, and that he could treat me as a vulnerable woman, confident that I'd react as one. And I did. The thought turned me on. His slap had been the most feminizing thing that had ever happened to me, the most pure forced feminization of my life. I still hadn't come, and now I reached down and adjusted myself.

At a stoplight back in the city, Felix glanced over and noticed. His hand finds me.

"You deserved that slap didn't you?" his tone velvety again. He's smiling in the red light of the traffic signal. He'd either been reading my thoughts, or had been lost in his own inverse, reciprocal version of them. "That's what happens to little bitches that get out of line, isn't it, Princess?"

I hold out my assent, unwilling to go that far. He pinches.

"Okay, yes! I deserved it."

"Good girl."

At the Riveria, Felix pulled to the side of the

parking lot and let the car idle. "Okay, Sweetie, here's what you're going to do to make this up to me. You're going to prove what a loyal girl you can be for your man. So you're going to call in the tip to report someone wearing a mask, just like Sally asked. But you're going to take note of Sally's outfit, and when you describe the supposed masker, you're going to describe Sally. That mess she calls her face is more fake-looking than any mask of mine."

Sally towers over a small crossdresser who's sitting beside me on the party bus. "Scoot yourself," Sally tells her, and when space is made, Sally plops down beside me with a grunt. A middle-aged trans woman, but only recently on hormones, I gather, attempts to spin around the stripper pole in the back of the bus, to a chorus of encouraging woos. Neon lights flash in time to the Rihanna song bumping from the back bench of the bus, which is itself a giant speaker beneath a flat-screen TV. Another woman, unsteady from either drink or too-high heels, attempts to join the first on the pole, and they both slide down into a heap on the bus floor. I join the others in a half-hearted woo.

Sally shoots me a glare. For a moment, I worry that Sally knows about Felix and me.

"What's wrong?" I ask, tentatively.

"Don't encourage her," says Sally with disgust, then in an only slightly more friendly tone calls out to the woman "Hey, your balls fell out." It's true, the second woman's short dress has come up in her tumble and a pair of shaven balls have escaped the side of her panties.

The woman stands and I recognize that I had talked to her at an earlier party. I can't remember her name, but she's a closeted, very very part-time cross-dresser, who sells flooring to large stores. Somewhat belligerently, she re-tucks her junk, and then as a sudden afterthought, swipes a glowstick from her seat, and stuffs it in her panties as well, so her crotch emits a muffled shine through the fabric. "Is that discreet enough for your delicate sensibilities?" she asks the bus, and gets a round of cackles in reply. Sally waves her hand as if casting a spell to make her disappear from sight.

The bus still hasn't left the Riviera. Girls are getting on and leaving, trading bottles to stock the party bus bar. "You know, this isn't the end for us, you and me," Sally says, "We're just starting our friend-

ship. And I'm going to be in Chicago this summer!"
She beams.

"Oh, that's cool, maybe I could drive to the city
for a night?"

"No, not just that," Sally says, "You said your
parents live in Chicago?"

"Yes." I can't bring myself to say more than that
on the subject of my parents.

"Hey, look at this," says Sally, and she rummages
around her purse for a moment and pulls out her
phone. Squinting, she looks down at it, and pulls up
something. "Is this your mom?" she asks, turning the
screen towards me.

A flush comes over me. It's my mom staring
at me on the dark of the party bus. It's so unex-
pected that I can't quite comprehend it, as if Alice,
wandering through Wonderland, came upon her
parents sipping tea with the Mad Hatter.

"What? Where did you get that?"

"You said your mom was so fierce, but I
googled her! She looks like a sweetheart!" She
zooms out the screen, and I see it's a corporate
headshot, from my mom's company website. No
one, so far as I know, has ever described my mom
as a sweetheart, including my dad.

"So, I have an idea," Sally goes on, "We'll do up your hair and all, and you can introduce your real self to them. Then you have me for support and they can ask any questions they have to a woman closer to their age! It'll be great, you'll see."

Sally wears a leather bustier, studded with metal rivets. The image of her sitting down with my mom would be like some kind of half-baked fan-fic crossover: two universes never meant to collide, that could only ever collide with horrible, ruinous results.

Now, Sally is talking about her own mother, how just after she transitioned, her car broke down, and called her mom for her AAA, but her mom insisted that she'd come herself. "You know what she said to me?" Sally said, "She said, 'I don't leave my child on the side of the highway no matter how you're dressed.' Mom hasn't seen me dressed like a man since. It'll be the same for you."

How well do I even know Sally? She found my mom on the Internet. Anyone can see she's lonely, and from her stories, I know she's unpredictable. Now she's googling my family? That's crazy. What if she decides to contact my mom?

"Sally, I don't know about." I say, "My parents aren't like yours."

"Parents are all the same," she says, confidently. "At the bottom of their heart, they love their kids."

"Sally," I say, "Have you seen any news stories about parents in the last ten years?" But she doesn't hear me. The choruses of wooing drown me out. Someone new gets on the bus. Someone dancing with a cup of liquor above her head, but I don't recognize her face. Then I see why I don't recognize her face. It's not really a face—it's a mask.

Felix is dancing, jointlessly, the breasts of his silicone body suit jiggling. The ass is more padded than last time, beneath a tight sequined red dress. A Jessica Rabbit outfit with proportions to match. He's by us now, at the pole, twerking against it, the lumps of his ass flopping to the beat. He spins around it, poses. The other girls on the bus, mostly part-time crossdressers, love it—so fun! They are wilding out on Felix, like bachelorettes at a male strip club revue. The flooring salesperson gets up and spanks Felix's ass, then grinds her glowing crotch into Felix's rear. I remember she said she had a wife and three kids— who know nothing about her dressing. Everyone is laughing, save Sally and me.

My own laugh dies on the vine. The picture of my mom glows behind my eyes, and when Felix turns, his mask points at my face. I cannot see him behind the bright blue eyes of the mask, just the dark slits, eye holes disguised in the curve of eyelid. Strangers, unpredictable strangers, all around me. Then a jiggle of movement and the blank eyes, the pert fake lips, swoop towards Sally, then pull back, long enough to be a taunt, but briefly enough to appear as mere accident.

The bus jerks into motion, glides through the parking lot and down the strip. Beside me, Sally glowers. Other girls are grinding on Felix now, laughing and falling over each other whenever the bus brakes. Even sitting, Sally keeps her shoulders rounded defensively, the tendons of her knuckles taut, still gripping her phone. The lights inside the bus match those around us—bright, gaudy, glitzy. Big costume jewels flash on earrings, rings, necklaces. The Bellagio fountains swirl by, water jets bopping to the beat of our bus. Girls shout out the sites: the Trop! The Luxor! Excalibur! The Strat! Now we're headed to the Las Vegas sign! We're gonna freak out the straights getting their wedding pictures!

Someone hands Felix a drink, and he pulls off his mask to drink it. And I'm so relieved. God, he's handsome. And he's just his normal self! His hair is a little disheveled, and he's sweating, but he leaves off the mask, and when he passes me by, he grins and winks. He's laughing now, throwing back his head and dancing with the other girls. I get up, dance my way near him, but not too close, wary of Sally's gaze. He sees me, grins, and I can't help but watch him. He looks so young now, happy and mischievous. I picture him as a young man, like the guys at college who dressed up for parties. Nothing scary, just a lark—the big boobs, the giant ass, nothing worse than parody, right?

He's watching me, and I know it, so I turn away, swing my hips. I've never danced this way in front of other people, but I know how it looks, I've done it for strangers on cam. I know how to move for sex. The driver announces that we all have to sit down while he's driving on the highway, but no one listens. Felix dances behind me, and leans in, "A good Princess listens to her Daddy. You know what you need to do." I keep my hips going.

When I turn to gauge the effect of my wiggles, I find Sally between him and me. "You need to sit down for the highway," she's shouting. "You have to sit down if we're going to get on the highway."

"What happens in Vegas stays in Vegas," shouts glow-crotch.

Now Sally snaps. "Sit the fuck down so the

man can drive us!"

The driver lowers the music just in time for Felix to say, too-loudly, "Once a narc, always a narc, huh girls?"

Sally doesn't sit at all. "Who told you I was a narc?" She and Felix are both in heels, but she's broader than him, taller than him. She's probably punched lots of people in her life, I realize.

But Felix laughs at her. "Maybe there's just something about you that says G-man." It was hard to tell whether or not he was intentionally emphasizing the "man."

The bus corners. Her hand shoots out for the stripper pole to catch her fall.

"Or maybe someone told me," Felix says, and gracefully, for being encased in silicone, takes a seat, "But I thought we were sitting down?"

Sally whips her head around. The other girls are following Felix's lead. Heavily, Sally plods back to our seat, holding the loops hanging from the ceiling for balance. She looks betrayed. Did I tell Felix she was a cop? I must have when I told him her plan. Was that not general knowledge?

When Sally sits back down beside me, I reach out to pat her shoulder, to ask if she's okay, but she shrugs me off. "Just make that phone call, okay?"

She pulls out her own phone. For a split-second, when she turns it on, my mom's face flashes across the screen, before Sally hits the home button. App icons zoom over my mom's face. Then Sally pulls up the number for Cosmopolitan Casino security, and texts it to me.

The bus pulls up to the Vegas sign, along with the three other party buses, and all the various stripes of trans tumble out, heels clacking on the cement, skirts pulled up, hundreds of girls flooding the scant space around the Vegas sign. Newly-weds posing for photos blanche, and approving car horns doppler by on either side of the highway around us.

As I get off the bus, Sally whispers, "Go!" I turn out from the parade of girls walking to the sign. There's a little lean-to at the edge of the parking lot, a glass wall sheltering screening out the noise of passing cars. Behind the lean-to I crouch, resting on my heels, out of view of the others.

I came out because I need something somehow in my life to change. I can't bear to live in stasis in Iowa much longer. For a moment, I hesitate, my mind oscillating between two images: Felix, whispering Princess as I danced for him, and Sally, with my mom lurking in her phone. The fun of forced femme fantasy, of clothes, of sexy power games versus the reality of transition. If I'm honest with myself, I know which one I want, maybe which one I've always wanted.

I pull up the number for Cosmopolitan security and hit the call button.

B ack in his room, Felix still hasn't removed his mask. He pushes me up against the wall, and his hands cup my crotch, then he pulls up my dress. I reach out to touch his arms, but they are cool, clammy, slightly sticky. It's the silicone skin. I keep forgetting, touching, then pulling back my fingers. His mask is close to my face, the huge eyes sightlessly watching me like two circles painted on a bobbing helium balloon. For an instant, I catch its smell—something like old paint and sweat, but he grabs my hair, and then everything is perfume from his wrist. He demands I squeeze his tits, so I reach for them, squeeze them through his dress, and he moans, then squeezes mine. I feel stupid, both of us squeezing falsies.

"That old bitch really got it, didn't she?" He asks, and the mask emits a mirthless dry laugh. "I didn't really think you'd do it. You're really the most obedient sissy I've ever had." He's been talking in a strange Minnie Mouse falsetto since he latched shut the door to the room.

I feel nauseated, and wish I'd brought my drink with me. I wish he'd stop bringing up Sally. My mind won't cooperate with me, it keeps loading the film of the three security guards waiting for Sally, on the lookout for clothing that matched my descriptions. Even with Felix pressed against me now, my mind plays the scene. They grabbed her. I saw them coming, I tried to get away, but she saw me, saw me dart away from her, and I know she understood. She watched me, her face actually a mask then, one of those Shakespearean masks of tragic comprehension. But then a security guard must have twisted her arm wrong, because she cried out, pulled away, and shoved the man. "I'm a cop too, asshole, that's not the way you do it."

The two other guards replaced the first, telling her variations of *calm down, sir, don't struggle, sir, we just need you to come with us.*

I couldn't hear what she said, because halfway through, the three of them tumble down. She landed on her boobs already bound tight in her bustier and her face contorted in pain. Then she went still as they pulled her up.

The crossdressers near her moved away. A few made half-hearted attempts at protesting transphobia, but when security men looked up, they shuffled back meekly. They've got wives, kids, and jobs. They can't afford an arrest. Sally was crying silently when they marched her off, her boobs half out of her top, but arms pinned so she couldn't adjust them, her head low in humiliation.

Then Felix was behind me, his mask off, whispering good job Princess and holding me by the hips, his crotch against my ass.

Now, I want to shake the image of Sally crying from my head. I want to enjoy this man for whom I've betrayed her. I need her out of my mind when he fucks me, as we both want him to do. But he won't take off his mask. He won't show himself to me. His falsetto grates on my ears, deep moans and grunts, then high-pitched dirty talk. I'm still squeezing his boobs, unwilling to touch the silicone skin when he pulls me from the wall and pushes me onto the bed. One heels falls off, and I'm on my back when his weight is on top of me. The silicone covering me like a blanket. His face comes close to mine, my nose tip to tip with the little bump of the mask's nose. I can't feel his own nose behind the bump. He's still for a moment. Then a tongue extrudes from the between the plump barely parted lips of the mask and finds my own lips, pushes its way into my mouth. We are both still for the barest moment. Then I lick his tongue back and tell myself that this is hot. I tell myself that this better than ending up like Sally. I tell myself that this is what I want.

About The Author

Torrey Peters is a writer living in Brooklyn. She has an MFA from the University of Iowa and her essays and stories have been published in *Prairie Schooner, Epoch, Brevity, McSweeney's, Fourth Genre, The Pinch, Shenandoah, Gawker.com,* and her work has been anthologized in *Best Travel Writing (2009, 2010), Tinderbox Editions, I'll Tell You Mine: 35 Years of the Iowa Nonfiction writing program, WaveForm: Twenty-First Century Essays By Women.* However, past publications aside, she's trans, and has concluded that the publishing industry doesn't serve trans women. So now, she just wants to give her work away for free to other trans girls. Get more of her work on Twitter, @torreypeters, or on her website, www.torreypeters.com